The Christmas Wishkeeper Chronicles

The Christmas Wishkeeper Chronicles

Matthew Edward Petchinsky

The Christmas Wishkeeper Chronicles
By: Matthew Petchinsky

Introduction: The Keeper of Holiday Dreams

In the heart of the world's collective imagination, nestled somewhere between wonder and belief, lies a mystical figure few have ever seen but whose presence is felt in every corner of the Christmas season—the Wishkeeper. Unlike the bustling elves in Santa's workshop or the radiant glow of holiday stars, the Wishkeeper is an enigmatic guardian, a being born from the very essence of hope and the purity of heartfelt dreams. Tasked with an extraordinary mission, the Wishkeeper safeguards the magic of Christmas by tending to the countless wishes made with sincerity, love, and the deepest of hearts.

The Wishkeeper's origins are as ancient as the tradition of Christmas itself. Long before stockings were hung by the fire or trees were adorned with twinkling lights, humanity yearned for connection, for miracles, and for the simple yet profound fulfillment of wishes. It is said that in the days when snowflakes first learned to dance and laughter first rang through frost-tipped evergreens, the magic of Christmas called forth a guardian—a silent protector to shield this sacred hope from the ravages of time, doubt, and despair.

The role of the Wishkeeper is one of profound responsibility and delicate precision. Every pure-hearted wish whispered into the frosty air, written in trembling letters to Santa, or hidden deep within a child's heart is collected and preserved. Some wishes, like the longing for a lost loved one's presence or the hope for peace in a troubled world, are too powerful to grant immediately. These are safeguarded in the ethereal chambers of the Wishkeeper's domain, patiently awaiting the perfect moment or aligning forces to make them reality. Other wishes, such as the dream of a cherished toy or a magical Christmas morning, are sent through shimmering currents of magic to be fulfilled, often in ways that weave unexpected joy into the lives of those who dared to dream.

Operating unseen, the Wishkeeper moves like a shadow through the festive glow of the season. By day, their work hums in the silent spaces between bustling crowds and caroling choirs, and by night, they walk the threshold between the tangible and the mystical. With a flick of their shimmering quill, they write wishes into the Book of Dreams, ensuring no heartfelt desire is overlooked. In their luminous satchel, they carry the hopes of millions, protecting them from the corrosive forces of doubt, greed, or malice that threaten the magic of Christmas.

But the Wishkeeper's work is far more than logistics—it is the very heartbeat of Christmas magic. They remind us that the season is not just about giving and receiving gifts but about believing in the impossible, cherishing connections, and holding space for miracles. The Wishkeeper ensures that the fragile threads of hope and joy are never lost, even in the darkest of times.

This tale unfolds in a world where the Wishkeeper's role is both celebrated and tested. From the moment a child makes their first earnest wish to the intricate weaving of destinies that bring people together in unexpected ways, the Wishkeeper's unseen hand guides the magic of Christmas. Along the way, they face trials that challenge the very essence of their purpose, encountering moments where even they must question the balance between granting wishes and teaching the lessons of hope, patience, and gratitude.

As you turn the pages of this story, prepare to be swept into an enchanting adventure that will warm your heart and ignite your sense of wonder. Journey with the Wishkeeper through realms of shimmering stardust, snow-covered forests, and glowing hearths, where every step reveals the extraordinary effort it takes to make Christmas dreams come true. This is a tale of belief, of courage, and of the quiet, relentless magic that binds us all in the spirit of the season.

Welcome to the world of the Wishkeeper—the Keeper of Holiday Dreams.

Chapter 1: The Last Keeper's Lament

Liora stood at the edge of her ethereal realm, a place shimmering with the faint remnants of magic that once pulsed like a heartbeat. Her domain, the Hall of Dreams, stretched infinitely, its vaulted ceilings adorned with cascading lights that reflected the essence of every wish ever made. Yet now, the lights flickered weakly, their brilliance dulled by the encroaching shadows of disbelief.

For over two centuries, Liora had been the steadfast guardian of Christmas wishes. She had witnessed eras of unyielding faith, where the mere thought of the holiday season filled hearts with warmth and homes with cheer. Wishes had poured in like rivers of light—children's heartfelt pleas for joy, parents' hopes for their families, and the unspoken yearnings of those who had no one else to confide in. But the tides had changed.

Materialism had crept into the holiday spirit like an insidious frost, numbing the purity of heartfelt dreams. Disbelief had spread, a toxin weakening the very magic Liora existed to protect. The modern world no longer believed in miracles, replacing wonder with cynicism and joy with lists of must-have possessions. The weight of this reality pressed heavily on her, a burden that even her immortal resolve struggled to bear.

In the quiet solitude of the Hall, Liora knelt before the Book of Dreams, the ancient ledger where every wish was recorded. Its once-glowing pages now seemed faded, the wishes sparse and scattered. She ran her delicate fingers over the parchment, tracing the ink of a child's recent plea—a wish for their parents to stop arguing. It glimmered faintly, a fragile hope struggling against the tide of despair.

"What have I become?" Liora whispered, her voice echoing in the cavernous hall. "A Wishkeeper without wishes? A guardian without believers?"

The silence answered her. Even the ever-present hum of magic that once filled the Hall was subdued, like a song fading into memory. She closed the Book gently, a deep ache in her chest. She had long known the prophecy etched into the foundation of her existence: a Wishkeeper without believers is powerless. It was a truth she had avoided facing, but now it loomed over her like a storm cloud.

For decades, Liora had tried to rekindle the fading spirit of Christmas. She had whispered hope into dreams, nudged hearts toward kindness, and even ventured into the mortal world disguised as a humble stranger, leaving tokens of magic for those who still dared to believe. Yet her efforts felt like pouring water into an endless void. The light of Christmas had grown too dim.

Her lament was interrupted by a strange, soft pulse emanating from the farthest corner of the Hall. Liora turned sharply, her senses alert. The sound was ancient and melodic, like a bell tolling in a distant memory. She followed it, her steps quickening as the pulse grew stronger.

She reached the Chamber of Prophecies, a secluded alcove deep within the Hall that she had not visited in decades. It housed the Scrolls of Continuance, sacred texts chronicling the destinies of the Wishkeepers and the ebb and flow of their magic. At the center of the chamber, a single scroll lay unrolled, its ink glowing faintly as if it had been waiting for her.

Liora hesitated before stepping closer. She knelt before the scroll, her eyes scanning its ancient script. Her breath caught as she read the words:

"When the last Keeper's light begins to fade, a child of starlight and wonder shall rise. From their belief, a new Keeper shall be born, and the magic of Christmas shall be restored to the world."

The prophecy struck her like a bolt of lightning. A new Wishkeeper? Her heart surged with a mixture of relief and sorrow. Relief that the magic she had dedicated her life to might not die, and sorrow at the realization that her time as Keeper was nearing its end.

But who was this "child of starlight and wonder"? Where would she find them? And would they truly have the strength to restore what seemed irrevocably lost?

Liora's fingers trembled as she touched the scroll, and in that moment, a vision erupted in her mind. She saw a child—a figure surrounded by a warm, radiant light, their eyes wide with unshakable belief. They stood at the center of a swirling storm of doubt, their tiny hands extended as if to grasp the fading threads of magic. Around them, the world flickered between despair and hope, as if their very presence was a battleground for the soul of Christmas.

The vision faded, leaving Liora breathless. She staggered back, clutching the edge of the pedestal for support. The Hall seemed to hum faintly, as though the magic itself had stirred in response to the prophecy's activation.

"The child," she whispered. "I must find the child."

For the first time in decades, a spark of purpose ignited within her. Though the path ahead was uncertain, and the weight of her fading magic pressed heavily on her, Liora knew she could not abandon the mission. She would seek out the child foretold in the prophecy. And in doing so, she might yet preserve the wonder and joy of Christmas—for the world and for herself.

With renewed determination, Liora returned to the Book of Dreams. She placed her hand over its cover, and for the first time in years, a faint glow pulsed beneath her palm.

"Let the search begin," she murmured.

Unbeknownst to her, far beyond the Hall of Dreams, in a small town blanketed by snow, a single child gazed out their frosted window. With a heart unspoiled by disbelief, they closed their eyes and made a wish—one so pure, it shimmered brighter than any Liora had seen in centuries.

Chapter 2: The Boy Who Believed

In a small, snow-covered town tucked between rolling hills, a boy named Ethan sat by the frosted window of his room, watching as snowflakes danced in the glow of the streetlights. His town, like many others, had begun its preparations for Christmas, but for Ethan, the usual warmth of the season felt far away. The laughter, the joy, the magic—it all seemed just out of reach. His family had been through a difficult year, one filled with arguments, loss, and a lingering sadness that no amount of holiday cheer could seem to dispel.

Ethan was a curious boy with a kind heart. Though only nine years old, he possessed a wisdom beyond his years, born of having to grow up too quickly. While other children in his class wished for the newest toys or the trendiest gadgets, Ethan's heart carried a different longing. What he wanted most wasn't something that could be wrapped in paper and placed beneath a tree—it was something far more precious.

Sitting by the window, Ethan closed his eyes and whispered his wish into the stillness of the night.

"I wish for my family to be happy again," he said softly, his breath fogging the glass. "Not just for Christmas... but for always."

Unbeknownst to Ethan, his words sent a ripple through the fabric of magic that bound the world. The purity of his wish, untouched by selfish desire, glowed brightly in the ether, a beacon in the vast sea of dimmed holiday dreams. It reached the Hall of Dreams like a shooting star piercing the darkness, and Liora, the last Wishkeeper, felt its pull immediately.

In her chamber, Liora had been preparing for her search for the prophesied child when she felt the surge of Ethan's wish. It was unlike any she had sensed in decades—pure, selfless, and unwavering. The glow of his wish illuminated the Hall, and for a moment, it was as though the ancient magic of Christmas was alive again.

"This is it," she whispered, her voice trembling with both hope and urgency. "The child of starlight and wonder."

Through the magical threads of the Book of Dreams, Liora peered into Ethan's life. She saw a boy who had faced more heartbreak than any child should endure—a boy who, despite the shadows in his home, still clung to the belief that things could be better. She saw his kindness in the small acts he performed daily: comforting his little sister when she cried, helping his mother with chores when she was too tired to move, and even shoveling the snow from his elderly neighbor's walkway without being asked. Ethan's heart was a wellspring of hope, and Liora knew she had found the one foretold in the prophecy.

But as she prepared to connect with him, a sinister presence stirred in the farthest reaches of the magical realm—a force she had hoped would never awaken again.

Far from the Hall of Dreams, in a realm of shadows and despair, the Grinchshade awakened. This malevolent entity, born from the remnants of broken dreams and lost hopes, had thrived for centuries on the disillusionment of humanity. It was a shapeless, writhing thing, its form shifting with every whisper of despair and every sigh of disappointment. The Grinchshade fed on the magic of Christmas by corrupting wishes, twisting them into something dark and destructive.

Ethan's wish, so pure and luminous, was like a siren call to the Grinchshade. It hungered for the light of his hope, knowing that by consuming it, it could extinguish the fragile spark of magic that Liora had fought so desperately to preserve.

"The boy's wish," the Grinchshade hissed, its voice a chilling echo that seemed to seep into the air itself. "So bright... so vulnerable. It will be mine to twist, to shatter."

The Grinchshade began to weave its dark magic, reaching out toward Ethan with tendrils of shadow. It sought to corrupt his wish by planting seeds of doubt and despair, twisting his longing for his family's happiness into fear and anger. It whispered lies into the night, hoping to turn his hope into bitterness and his belief into disbelief.

Ethan, oblivious to the brewing conflict, spent the following day trying to bring some semblance of Christmas spirit back into his home.

He decorated a small tree in his living room, its ornaments mismatched and worn but placed with care. He baked cookies with his younger sister, Lily, despite their mother's distracted demeanor. Ethan's father had been distant lately, retreating into his work and barely speaking to the family. Ethan felt the weight of their fractured home but refused to let it crush him.

That evening, as he stared at the tree's twinkling lights, Ethan felt an inexplicable sense of warmth and comfort. It was faint but undeniable, like a gentle whisper telling him he wasn't alone. Liora, watching from the Hall of Dreams, had sent him a small blessing—a touch of magic to strengthen his hope and shield him from the Grinchshade's influence.

But the Grinchshade was relentless. It slithered into the edges of Ethan's dreams that night, manifesting as dark, unsettling images. In these nightmares, Ethan saw his family arguing, the lights of Christmas extinguished, and his wish crumbling into ashes. He woke with a start, his heart pounding, the shadows of doubt creeping into his mind.

Yet even in the face of these nightmares, Ethan's belief held firm. He clutched the small star ornament he had hung at the top of the tree—a family heirloom his mother had given him—and whispered to himself, "Christmas is about love. I won't stop believing."

Liora knew time was of the essence. The Grinchshade's presence was growing stronger, and if she didn't intervene, Ethan's wish—and the prophecy—could be lost forever. She prepared to leave the Hall of Dreams for the mortal world, her powers flickering as she gathered what little strength remained.

As she stepped through the portal that bridged their worlds, Liora whispered a vow: "I will protect your wish, Ethan. No matter the cost."

And so, the stage was set for a battle between light and darkness, hope and despair. Ethan, the boy who believed, and Liora, the last Wishkeeper, would face the Grinchshade together in a fight to preserve the magic of Christmas and the power of dreams. But the journey ahead would test their courage, their faith, and their very hearts in ways neither of them could have imagined.

Chapter 3: The Journey to the Star Forge

The moment Liora stepped into Ethan's world, the air around her seemed to hum with possibility. Cloaked in a shimmer of magic that rendered her invisible to others, she stood at the foot of Ethan's bed, watching the boy sleep. His room was modest, with hand-me-down furniture and the faint glow of Christmas lights taped to the wall. Clutched in his small hand was the star ornament he treasured, its edges worn from years of use. Liora's heart ached as she saw the faint traces of doubt on his brow, a shadow planted by the Grinchshade's sinister whispers.

"Ethan," she said softly, her voice lilting like a melody in a dream.

The boy stirred, his eyes fluttering open. When he saw Liora, his gaze widened—not in fear, but in awe. She stood before him, her form glowing faintly with a soft golden light. Her long, silvery hair seemed to move as though caught in an eternal breeze, and her deep, violet eyes carried the weight of countless Christmases past.

"Who... who are you?" Ethan asked, sitting up and clutching the star ornament tighter.

"I am Liora," she said, her voice warm and steady. "A Wishkeeper. I am here because of the wish you made—the one so pure and bright that it reached the very heart of Christmas magic."

Ethan's confusion gave way to curiosity. "You heard my wish?"

"Indeed, and it is unlike any I have heard in centuries," Liora replied. "But we must act quickly. There is a dark force called the Grinchshade. It seeks to twist your wish into something terrible, to feed on your hope and destroy the magic of Christmas."

Ethan frowned, his small shoulders straightening with resolve. "What can I do? I just want my family to be happy again."

Liora smiled, kneeling to meet his gaze. "You can help me protect your wish by coming with me to the Star Forge, the sacred place where all pure-hearted wishes are forged into reality. But the journey will not be easy. It will test your courage, your selflessness, and your belief. Are you ready for such a task?"

The boy hesitated for only a moment before nodding. "I'll do it."

Into the Magical Realms

Liora extended her hand, and when Ethan took it, the room around them dissolved into a swirl of light and color. Ethan gasped as they stepped into a shimmering landscape filled with floating islands, crystalline bridges, and rivers of starlight. The air was thick with the scent of pine and peppermint, and the distant sound of carolers echoed faintly, carried on the wind.

"This is the Luminal Path," Liora explained. "It connects our world to the Star Forge, but it is not without its dangers."

As they walked, the Luminal Path began to shift and twist, forming challenges that reflected Ethan's inner doubts and fears. The first test came in the form of an endless, icy forest, its trees dark and foreboding. The ground was slick with frost, and shadows danced between the trunks.

"We must move quickly," Liora urged. "The Grinchshade's presence grows stronger the longer we linger."

Ethan hesitated, his breath visible in the freezing air. "What if we get lost?"

"You must trust yourself," Liora said. "The path will guide us if your heart remains true."

Ethan took a deep breath and stepped forward. As he walked, the shadows seemed to close in, whispering fears and doubts: *Your family will never be happy. You are too small to make a difference.* He clutched the star ornament tightly and whispered to himself, "I believe. I believe in Christmas."

The shadows recoiled, and the forest began to glow faintly. Liora smiled. "Well done, Ethan. Your belief strengthens the path."

The Bridge of Giving

Their next challenge came at the Bridge of Giving, a magnificent structure made of shimmering gold and silver that spanned a chasm filled with swirling darkness. As they approached, a figure appeared—a little girl, crying and clutching a broken toy.

Ethan hesitated. "Who is she?"

"A test," Liora replied. "Her plight is real, but whether you help her is your choice."

Ethan approached the girl. "What's wrong?"

"My toy," she sobbed. "It's broken, and I have nothing else to play with."

Ethan looked at the star ornament in his hand. It was his most treasured possession, the last remnant of his family's happier times. He glanced back at Liora, who said nothing, her expression unreadable.

With a deep breath, Ethan knelt and offered the ornament to the girl. "Here. It's not a toy, but it's very special. Maybe it can make you happy."

The girl took the star, and as she did, her form shimmered and dissolved into light. The bridge lit up, the path ahead solidifying.

"You have shown selflessness," Liora said, pride in her voice. "The magic of the Forge grows stronger with every step you take."

The Grinchshade's Attack

As they neared the Star Forge, the air grew heavy with malice. The Grinchshade appeared in its true form—a writhing mass of shadows with glowing red eyes, its voice a cacophony of despair.

"You cannot stop me," it hissed. "The boy's wish is mine to twist, his hope mine to consume."

Ethan stepped forward, fear coursing through him but courage keeping him steady. "You can't have my wish. I won't let you!"

The Grinchshade lunged, its tendrils reaching for Ethan, but Liora intervened, her hands glowing with golden light. "Ethan, remember what you believe in! Speak your truth!"

Ethan closed his eyes and shouted, "I believe in Christmas! I believe in love and hope and family!"

The words ignited a burst of light from the path itself, forcing the Grinchshade to retreat, screaming in agony. The darkness began to dissipate, and the Star Forge appeared on the horizon—a towering structure of light and crystal, radiating warmth and magic.

Arrival at the Star Forge

Ethan and Liora stood before the Star Forge, its massive gates opening to welcome them. Inside, the walls glowed with the light of countless wishes, each represented by a star-like orb floating in the air.

Liora turned to Ethan. "Place your hand on the Forge, and let your wish take form."

Ethan did as she instructed, and as he whispered his wish again, the Forge erupted in light. His hope and belief filled the chamber, and for a moment, he felt the weight of every pure-hearted wish ever made. The star ornament he had given away reappeared in his hand, glowing with new brilliance.

"You have done well," Liora said, her voice filled with emotion. "But the journey is not over. The Grinchshade is not defeated—it is merely weakened. Your belief will continue to be tested."

Ethan nodded, clutching the star. "I won't give up."

And as the Forge solidified his wish into reality, Ethan realized that the magic of Christmas wasn't just in the granting of wishes—it was in the courage to believe, even when the world tried to take that belief away.

Chapter 4: The Grinchshade's Gambit

The Star Forge glowed with radiant light, its crystalline walls pulsing with the energy of countless wishes made over generations. Ethan stood in awe, feeling the power of the Forge resonating within him. For a moment, he felt invincible, as if the magic of Christmas itself had chosen him to carry its light. Liora, standing beside him, allowed herself a small smile. But her expression quickly hardened, her eyes narrowing as the air around them grew colder, heavier.

"It's here," she murmured.

Before Ethan could ask what she meant, a chilling laugh echoed through the Forge. The light dimmed, shadows creeping across the walls like an encroaching tide. From the darkness, the Grinchshade emerged, its form a swirling mass of malevolent energy, its crimson eyes burning with hatred.

"Well, well," it hissed, its voice dripping with malice. "The last Wishkeeper and her little protégé. How quaint."

Ethan stepped back, clutching the glowing star ornament in his hand. "What do you want?" he demanded, his voice trembling but defiant.

"What do I want?" The Grinchshade chuckled, the sound like ice scraping against stone. "I want what I've always wanted—to extinguish the light of Christmas hope and plunge this world into despair. And now, thanks to you, boy, I can destroy the Star Forge and end the Wishkeeper lineage forever."

Liora stepped protectively in front of Ethan, her hands glowing with golden energy. "You will not harm him, Grinchshade. Nor will you touch the Forge."

The entity laughed again, its form expanding to fill the chamber. "You're weaker than you've ever been, Liora. The magic of belief fades, and with it, your strength. You cannot stop me."

Liora's glow faltered for a moment, and Ethan noticed the weariness in her eyes. But she straightened, her voice steady. "Perhaps I am weaker, but I am not alone. And you underestimate the power of hope."

The Grinchshade sneered. "Hope? Let's test that, shall we?"

A Test of Courage

The Grinchshade lashed out with tendrils of shadow, aiming for Ethan. Liora raised a shield of light, but the force of the attack sent her stumbling. Ethan's heart raced as he watched her struggle to maintain her defenses. The entity's power was overwhelming, and for the first time, he felt the crushing weight of responsibility. He wasn't just a boy anymore—he was a budding Wishkeeper, and the fate of the Forge rested on his shoulders.

The Grinchshade's voice echoed in his mind, a whisper of doubt. *You're too small, too weak. You don't belong here. Give up, and I'll spare you.*

Ethan clenched his fists, refusing to succumb to the darkness. "I won't let you win!" he shouted, his voice carrying through the chamber. He felt a warmth in his chest, the same warmth he had felt when he made his wish. It spread through him, igniting a spark of courage.

Liora turned to him, her voice urgent. "Ethan, the Forge responds to those who believe. Trust in your heart, and it will guide you."

Ethan nodded, gripping the star ornament tightly. Closing his eyes, he focused on the wish that had brought him here—the pure, selfless desire for his family's happiness. As he did, the star began to glow brighter, its light pushing back the shadows.

The Grinchshade hissed in anger, its tendrils recoiling. "You think a child's hope can stop me?"

The Forge Awakens

Ethan felt a surge of energy flow through him, as if the Forge itself was answering his call. Around him, the chamber began to glow once more, the light growing stronger with every passing second. He raised the star ornament, and beams of light shot out from it, forming a protective barrier around the Forge.

The Grinchshade roared, its form flickering. "You meddling fool! You cannot protect the Forge forever!"

Liora joined Ethan, her hands glowing as she lent her remaining strength to the barrier. "You're stronger than you realize, Ethan," she said, her voice steady despite her exhaustion. "The Forge has chosen you. Use its power."

Ethan closed his eyes again, allowing the warmth of the Forge to fill him. He saw visions of past Wishkeepers, their courage and belief shining like beacons through the ages. He understood now—being a Wishkeeper wasn't just about granting wishes; it was about protecting the hope that made them possible.

"I won't let you destroy Christmas!" Ethan declared, his voice ringing with newfound strength. He raised the star ornament high, and the Forge responded, its light erupting in a dazzling display.

The Grinchshade's Gambit

But the Grinchshade was not finished. With a guttural growl, it shifted its focus, reaching into the shadows to reveal a twisted plan. Before Ethan's eyes, a dark mirror-like portal appeared, showing an image of his family. In the vision, they were arguing, their faces filled with anger and sadness.

"Look at them," the Grinchshade sneered. "Even now, they falter. Your wish is nothing but a fantasy, boy. Your family's happiness is beyond saving."

Ethan felt a pang of doubt, the image stirring his deepest fears. But Liora placed a hand on his shoulder, her touch grounding him.

"Do not let it deceive you," she said firmly. "The Grinchshade thrives on despair, but your belief can rewrite the future."

Ethan focused on the image, replacing the despair with the vision of his family laughing together, their home filled with warmth and joy. The image in the portal wavered, then shattered, the shards dissolving into light.

"No!" the Grinchshade screamed, its form shrinking as the Forge's light intensified.

The Final Stand

Ethan took a step forward, his confidence unshaken. "You can't win, Grinchshade. I believe in my wish, and I believe in Christmas."

With those words, the star ornament erupted in a burst of golden light, its energy channeling directly into the Forge. The chamber trembled as the Forge activated fully, its power overwhelming the Grinchshade. The shadows writhed and screamed, retreating into the void.

"You haven't seen the last of me!" the Grinchshade snarled as it vanished, its presence reduced to a faint whisper in the distance.

A New Wishkeeper

As the light of the Forge settled, Liora knelt beside Ethan, her expression one of pride and relief. "You did it, Ethan. You've proven yourself worthy."

Ethan looked at the star ornament, now glowing with a steady, comforting light. "Does this mean... I'm a Wishkeeper?"

Liora nodded. "The Forge has chosen you to carry on its legacy. You have the courage, selflessness, and belief needed to protect the magic of Christmas."

Ethan smiled, his heart swelling with pride. But he knew the journey wasn't over. The Grinchshade would return, and there were countless wishes still waiting to be fulfilled.

As they left the Forge, the light of Christmas hope shining brighter than ever, Ethan knew one thing for certain: he was ready to face whatever challenges lay ahead. For the first time in a long time, the world had a new Wishkeeper—and with him, the promise that the magic of Christmas would endure.

Chapter 5: The First Wishkeeper of a New Era

The Star Forge stood in radiant silence, its crystal walls glowing with a renewed brilliance that had not been seen in centuries. The battle with the Grinchshade had left the air heavy with the lingering echoes of its cries, but those echoes were fading now, replaced by the warm hum of the Forge's magic. Ethan stood in the center of the chamber, the star ornament in his hand shining like a miniature sun, its light resonating with the energy of the Forge. He had done it—he had saved the magic of Christmas.

Liora watched him with a mixture of pride and bittersweet longing. She could feel the weight of centuries lifting from her shoulders, the duty she had carried for so long now passing into the hands of a new Wishkeeper. Ethan's journey had been one of courage and selflessness, and she knew in her heart that he was ready to carry on the legacy.

"You've done something truly remarkable, Ethan," Liora said, her voice soft yet steady. "You've proven that even in the darkest times, belief can shine brighter than any shadow. The Star Forge has chosen you to be the first Wishkeeper of a new era."

Ethan turned to her, his expression a mixture of excitement and uncertainty. "But... what does that mean? What do I do now?"

Accepting the Mantle

Liora stepped closer, kneeling so they were eye level. "Being a Wishkeeper is not just about granting wishes, Ethan. It's about protecting the hope that makes them possible. The magic of Christmas isn't in toys or decorations—it's in the belief that miracles can happen, that kindness and love can triumph even in the hardest times. Your role is to nurture that belief, to ensure that every pure-hearted wish is given the chance to shine."

Ethan nodded slowly, his grip tightening on the star ornament. "I'll do my best."

"You will," Liora said with a gentle smile. "But remember, you won't be alone. The Forge will guide you, and its magic will grow stronger as more people begin to believe again. Your courage and actions will inspire others."

As if responding to her words, the Forge pulsed with light, sending a ripple of warmth through the chamber. Ethan felt the energy flow into him, filling him with a sense of purpose. The star ornament in his hand transformed, its shape shifting into a radiant pendant that glowed softly against his chest.

"This is your connection to the Forge," Liora explained. "Through it, you can sense wishes, protect them, and channel the magic needed to fulfill them. It is both your tool and your responsibility."

Liora's Farewell

As the magic of the Forge solidified Ethan's new role, Liora felt a subtle but profound change within herself. The bond that had tied her to the Forge for centuries was loosening, replaced by a lightness she hadn't felt in lifetimes. Her time as a Wishkeeper was over.

"I'm so proud of you, Ethan," she said, her voice tinged with both joy and sorrow. "You've not only saved the Forge but given it a future. The Wishkeeper legacy lives on through you."

Ethan looked at her, alarmed. "Wait... what's happening? You're not leaving, are you?"

Liora smiled, the glow of her form becoming brighter. "My duty is complete, Ethan. For over two centuries, I've carried this responsibility, but now it's time for me to rest. The magic of the Forge has chosen you as its new guardian, and I couldn't ask for a better successor."

Tears welled in Ethan's eyes. "But I still need you."

"You've always had everything you need, Ethan," Liora replied gently. "Your courage, your kindness, and your belief have brought you here. Trust in yourself, and in the magic of Christmas. I will always be a part of this legacy, just as every Wishkeeper before me has been."

With those words, Liora's form began to shimmer and rise, her essence dissolving into a cascade of golden light. Ethan watched as the light ascended, merging with the Forge's energy, leaving behind a sense of peace and warmth.

A New Era Begins

Ethan stood alone in the Star Forge, the pendant on his chest glowing softly. For a moment, he felt the weight of the responsibility before him, but as he looked around the radiant chamber, he realized he wasn't truly alone. The magic of the Forge, the legacy of Wishkeepers past, and the hope of countless believers were with him.

Stepping to the center of the Forge, he placed his hand on its crystalline core. A surge of energy coursed through him, and he felt the presence of wishes all over the world—small wishes, big wishes, and everything in between. Each one was a thread of light, connecting him to the hearts of those who still dared to dream.

The pendant pulsed, and Ethan instinctively knew what to do. Closing his eyes, he focused on a single wish—a child's wish for their parents to have enough money for Christmas presents. The Forge responded, sending a wave of magic that would bring unexpected generosity to the family.

As he opened his eyes, Ethan felt a deep sense of fulfillment. He had taken his first step as a Wishkeeper, and it felt right.

Inspiring Belief

Word of the renewed magic of Christmas began to spread in ways Ethan couldn't have predicted. Families reunited, acts of kindness flourished, and the holiday spirit seemed to grow stronger with each passing day. Ethan's efforts as a Wishkeeper, though unseen by most, touched countless lives, rekindling the belief that had been fading for so long.

Even his own family felt the change. The warmth and love that had once seemed so distant began to return, their home filled with laughter and joy once more. Ethan's wish, the one that had started it all, had come true—not through magic alone, but through the hope and love he had nurtured within himself.

The Legacy Lives On

As the days turned into weeks and the Christmas season unfolded, Ethan grew into his role as a Wishkeeper. The Star Forge became his sanctuary, a place where he could connect with the magic of belief and the dreams of those he sought to protect. Though the Grinchshade was weakened, Ethan knew it wasn't gone entirely. He remained vigilant, ready to face any challenge that threatened the light of Christmas.

And somewhere, in the peaceful afterlife where former Wishkeepers found rest, Liora watched over him, her heart filled with pride. The legacy she had carried for so long was safe, and the magic of Christmas, once on the brink of extinction, shone brighter than ever.

Ethan, the first Wishkeeper of a new era, had proven that even in the face of darkness, belief could prevail—and that the magic of Christmas wasn't just a tradition but a force of hope that could light the world for generations to come.

Appendix A: The Lore of the Wishkeepers

The mythology of the Wishkeepers is as intricate and wondrous as the magic they protect. Born from the collective hopes of humanity, the Wishkeepers are guardians of the holiday spirit, tasked with safeguarding the purity of Christmas wishes and ensuring that the magic of belief endures through the ages.

Origins of the Wishkeepers

The legend of the Wishkeepers begins in the earliest days of human storytelling, long before Christmas as we know it. In ancient times, when winter was a season of harsh survival, people turned to the stars for guidance, seeking hope and light in the darkness. It was said that when the first pure-hearted wish was made—a child's prayer for warmth and love—the magic of belief was born. This wish ignited the creation of the Star Forge, a celestial nexus where wishes of pure intent could be transformed into reality.

The magic of the Forge, however, was fragile and vulnerable to corruption. To protect this sacred force, the first Wishkeeper was chosen from among humanity—a selfless soul who embodied hope and courage. Over time, as belief in the power of wishes grew, the lineage of Wishkeepers was established, with each generation passing their knowledge and duties to the next.

Roles of the Wishkeepers

Wishkeepers serve as the protectors, guides, and champions of the magic of Christmas. Their roles are multi-faceted, requiring courage, wisdom, and a deep understanding of human hearts. The key responsibilities of a Wishkeeper include:

1. **Collecting Wishes**
   - Wishes made with pure hearts are collected through the magical currents of belief that flow through the world. These wishes manifest as glowing orbs of light, each unique in size, color, and intensity, reflecting the depth and sincerity of the wish.
   - Wishes are drawn to the Star Forge, where they are cataloged and preserved in the **Book of Dreams**, an ancient ledger containing the essence of every wish ever made.

2. **Protecting the Magic**
   - Wishkeepers safeguard the Forge and its magic from entities like the Grinchshade, which seek to corrupt and destroy belief. This requires constant vigilance and the ability to shield wishes from dark influences.

3. **Fulfilling Wishes**
   - Not all wishes can be fulfilled immediately. Wishkeepers must discern the right time and method for each wish to be granted, ensuring that it aligns with the greater balance of magic and the best interests of the wisher.

4. **Inspiring Belief**
   - A Wishkeeper's most important role is to inspire belief in others. Without belief, the magic of the Forge weakens, leaving wishes unfulfilled and the light of Christmas dimmed. Wishkeepers accomplish this through acts of

kindness, courage, and quiet miracles that reignite the spark of hope in human hearts.

The Star Forge

The Star Forge is the heart of the Wishkeeper mythology—a celestial sanctuary where the magic of Christmas is channeled, amplified, and preserved. Located in a plane of existence between the mortal world and the realm of magic, the Forge is both a physical and metaphysical construct.

- **Structure and Design**
  The Forge appears as a crystalline fortress, its towering spires reaching into an endless expanse of starlight. Its central chamber houses the **Core Crystal**, a pulsating orb of energy that acts as the nexus for all Christmas magic. Surrounding the Core are the **Chambers of Wishes**, where wish orbs float in an ethereal ballet, awaiting fulfillment.
- **Symbol of the Forge**
  The primary symbol of the Star Forge is a six-pointed star encircled by an infinite loop, representing the eternal cycle of belief and the transformative power of hope.

Wishkeeper Tools

Wishkeepers are equipped with magical tools that enable them to perform their duties and connect with the Star Forge. Each tool is imbued with the essence of the Forge, making it a powerful extension of the Wishkeeper's will.

1. **The Star Pendant**
   - Every Wishkeeper is given a **Star Pendant**, a glowing artifact that serves as their link to the Forge. The pendant allows the Wishkeeper to sense wishes, channel the Forge's magic, and protect their charges from dark forces.
2. **The Book of Dreams**
   - This ancient ledger records every wish made with pure intent. Wishkeepers use the Book to track and prioritize wishes, ensuring that none are forgotten.
3. **The Wand of Light**
   - A symbolic tool used to channel magic, the Wand of Light can emit beams of energy to combat darkness, heal broken wishes, or illuminate the path for those lost in despair.
4. **The Shimmer Cloak**
   - A shimmering, silver cloak that allows Wishkeepers to move unseen among mortals. It also provides protection against dark entities like the Grinchshade.

The Grinchshade: An Ancient Foe

The Grinchshade, a dark and malevolent force, represents the antithesis of the Wishkeepers' mission. It is a shadowy entity born from broken dreams and shattered hopes, thriving on disbelief and despair. Its goal is to corrupt the magic of Christmas by twisting wishes into curses and extinguishing belief.

The Grinchshade's symbol is a fractured star surrounded by jagged shadows, a stark contrast to the harmonious design of the Forge's emblem. Its presence weakens the Star Forge, making the role of the Wish-keepers all the more vital.

The Legacy of Belief

The Wishkeeper mythology emphasizes the enduring power of belief. Wishes are not merely granted through magic—they are manifestations of the wisher's faith in something greater than themselves. The Wishkeepers act as guardians of this faith, ensuring that the magic of Christmas remains a beacon of hope, even in the darkest times.

Diagram of the Star Forge

◈

◈ ◈

●

◈ ◈

◈

[Core Crystal]

- Radiates light and energy that powers the Forge.

- Surrounded by Chambers of Wishes.

[Six-Pointed Star Symbol]

- Represents harmony, balance, and the cycle of belief.

[Infinite Loop]

- Encircles the Star, symbolizing the eternal nature of hope.

The Wishkeepers are more than guardians of magic; they are stewards of humanity's capacity to dream, believe, and hope. With Ethan as the first Wishkeeper of a new era, the legacy of the Star Forge and the magic of Christmas shine brighter than ever, promising that no wish made with a pure heart will ever be forgotten.

Appendix B: The Grinchshade Chronicles

The Grinchshade is one of the most feared entities in the mythos of the Wishkeepers, embodying the darkness that threatens to extinguish the light of belief. Its origins are shrouded in mystery, but its impact on the magic of Christmas is profound and deeply tied to the very essence of despair, greed, and broken dreams.

Origins of the Grinchshade

The Grinchshade was born in a time of disillusionment and loss, when the purity of belief began to waver in the face of cynicism. Legend says that its first manifestation occurred centuries ago, when a community, once vibrant with holiday cheer, fell into conflict and despair over greed and envy. The collective negativity of their broken dreams coalesced into a formless shadow, and thus, the Grinchshade came into existence.

Unlike the Wishkeepers, whose creation stems from hope and selflessness, the Grinchshade thrives on the absence of belief. It is a being forged not by light but by the void left when hope is abandoned. Over time, it has grown stronger as the world has struggled with materialism, greed, and the erosion of pure-hearted faith.

Nature and Abilities

The Grinchshade is not a physical being but an amalgamation of despair, corrupted wishes, and disbelief. Its powers are vast, making it a formidable adversary for the Wishkeepers and the Star Forge.

1. **Manifestations of Despair**
   - The Grinchshade's form is fluid and ever-changing, appearing as a swirling mass of shadows with piercing red eyes. It can assume terrifying shapes to exploit the fears of its victims.
   - It uses whispers to sow doubt and despair, often appearing in dreams or moments of vulnerability to twist hope into fear.

2. **Corruption of Wishes**
   - The Grinchshade's primary weapon is its ability to corrupt pure-hearted wishes. By feeding on the doubt or fear of the wisher, it can turn a wish into something harmful or hollow.
   - It thrives on the energy of broken dreams, growing stronger with each wish it distorts or destroys.

3. **Weakening the Star Forge**
   - The Grinchshade targets the magic of the Star Forge directly, seeking to sever the connection between belief and the Forge's power. When belief falters, the Grinchshade's influence spreads, dimming the light of Christmas.

4. **Temporal Displacement**
   - The Grinchshade exists partially outside the flow of time, allowing it to appear in multiple locations simultaneously or retreat to its shadowy realm when threatened.

5. **Creation of Minions**
   - The Grinchshade can summon shadow-like minions called **Dream Wraiths**, which act as extensions of its will. These wraiths are sent to stalk and torment those who still be-

lieve, weakening their faith before the Grinchshade confronts them directly.

Motivations and Goals

The Grinchshade's ultimate goal is to extinguish the magic of Christmas and plunge the world into eternal despair. It views the light of belief as a direct threat to its existence and will stop at nothing to snuff it out. Its motivations stem not from a need for power but from a deep, intrinsic hatred of hope and joy.

In its twisted logic, the Grinchshade sees belief as a fragile illusion, one that it seeks to dismantle by exposing humanity's darker tendencies. It preys on greed, envy, and self-interest, amplifying these emotions to erode the foundation of hope that powers the Star Forge.

The Grinchshade's Weaknesses

Despite its formidable abilities, the Grinchshade is not invincible. Its power is directly tied to the strength of disbelief and despair, meaning it can be weakened when confronted with pure-hearted belief and acts of selflessness.

1. **The Light of Belief**
   - The Grinchshade cannot withstand direct exposure to the untainted magic of belief, which is why it seeks to corrupt wishes before they can manifest fully.
2. **The Star Forge**
   - As the source of Christmas magic, the Star Forge emits a light that can repel the Grinchshade, particularly when powered by strong, unshaken faith.
3. **The Courage of a Wishkeeper**
   - Wishkeepers, who embody the magic of belief, are the Grinchshade's natural adversaries. Their connection to the Forge allows them to counter its influence, provided their faith remains unbroken.

Potential Future Adversaries

While the Grinchshade is the primary antagonist in the Wishkeeper mythology, the magical realm surrounding the Star Forge holds other potential threats. These adversaries, each representing a different aspect of humanity's struggles, could emerge in future tales.

1. **The Frostbinder**
   - A being born from cold indifference, the Frostbinder seeks to freeze the hearts of mortals, replacing warmth and joy with apathy. It thrives in environments where people have become emotionally distant, feeding on the chill of neglect.

2. **The Emberkin**
   - Representing greed and unchecked ambition, the Emberkin manifests as a fiery entity that incinerates anything it cannot control. It targets those who desire power at the expense of others, amplifying their destructive tendencies.

3. **The Echo of Sorrow**
   - A spectral entity formed from collective grief, the Echo of Sorrow traps people in their past, preventing them from moving forward. Its whispers drown out the voices of hope, leaving only regret and longing.

4. **The Nightveil**
   - A cunning adversary, the Nightveil represents the power of lies and deception. It specializes in creating illusions, causing individuals to doubt their reality and abandon their beliefs.

5. **The Hollow King**
   - An ancient rival of the Wishkeepers, the Hollow King rules over a realm of lost and forgotten wishes. He seeks to claim the Star Forge for himself, believing that wishes should serve the powerful rather than the pure-hearted.

Symbol of the Grinchshade

The Grinchshade's symbol is a fractured star surrounded by jagged, chaotic lines, representing the destruction of unity and hope. This symbol contrasts sharply with the harmonious design of the Star Forge's emblem, emphasizing the Grinchshade's role as the antithesis of belief.

The Eternal Conflict

The struggle between the Wishkeepers and the Grinchshade is a reflection of the timeless battle between hope and despair. While the Grinchshade's defeat at the hands of Ethan and Liora marked a turning point, its essence lingers, waiting for moments of vulnerability to rise again.

As the first Wishkeeper of a new era, Ethan not only carries the legacy of the Star Forge but also the responsibility of defending it against future threats. The Grinchshade may return, or new adversaries may rise, but the core message of the Wishkeeper mythology remains unchanged: belief is the most powerful magic of all, and even in the darkest times, it has the strength to prevail.

<u>Message from the Author:</u>

I hope you enjoyed this book, I love astrology and knew there was not a book such as this out on the shelf. I love metaphysical items as well. Please check out my other books:

-Life of Government Benefits

-My life of Hell

-My life with Hydrocephalus

-Red Sky

-World Domination:Woman's rule

-World Domination:Woman's Rule 2: The War

-Life and Banishment of Apophis: book 1

-The Kidney Friendly Diet

-The Ultimate Hemp Cookbook

-Creating a Dispensary(legally)

-Cleanliness throughout life: the importance of showering from childhood to adulthood.

-Strong Roots: The Risks of Overcoddling children

-Hemp Horoscopes: Cosmic Insights and Earthly Healing

- Celestial Hemp Navigating the Zodiac: Through the Green Cosmos

-Astrological Hemp: Aligning The Stars with Earth's Ancient Herb

-The Astrological Guide to Hemp: Stars, Signs, and Sacred Leaves

-Green Growth: Innovative Marketing Strategies for your Hemp Products and Dispensary

-Cosmic Cannabis

-Astrological Munchies

-Henry The Hemp

-Zodiacal Roots: The Astrological Soul Of Hemp

- **Green Constellations: Intersection of Hemp and Zodiac**

-Hemp in The Houses: An astrological Adventure Through The Cannabis Galaxy

-Galactic Ganja Guide

Heavenly Hemp

Zodiac Leaves

Doctor Who Astrology

Cannastrology

Stellar Satvias and Cosmic Indicas

<u>Celestial Cannabis: A Zodiac Journey</u>

AstroHerbology: The Sky and The Soil: Volume 1

AstroHerbology:Celestial Cannabis:Volume 2

Cosmic Cannabis Cultivation

The Starry Guide to Herbal Harmony: Volume 1

The Starry Guide to Herbal Harmony: Cannabis Universe: Volume 2

Yugioh Astrology: Astrological Guide to Deck, Duels and more

Nightmare Mansion: Echoes of The Abyss

Nightmare Mansion 2: Legacy of Shadows

Nightmare Mansion 3: Shadows of the Forgotten

Nightmare Mansion 4: Echoes of the Damned

The Life and Banishment of Apophis: Book 2

Nightmare Mansion: Halls of Despair

<u>Healing with Herb: Cannabis and Hydrocephalus</u>

<u>Planetary Pot: Aligning with Astrological Herbs: Volume 1</u>

Fast Track to Freedom: 30 Days to Financial Independence Using AI, Assets, and Agile Hustles

<u>Cosmic Hemp Pathways</u>

How to Become Financially Free in 30 Days: 10,000 Paths to Prosperity

Zodiacal Herbage: Astrological Insights: Volume 1

Nightmare Mansion: Whispers in the Walls

The Daleks Invade Atlantis

Henry the hemp and Hydrocephalus

10X The Kidney Friendly Diet

Cannabis Universe: Adult coloring book

Hemp Astrology: The Healing Power of the Stars

Zodiacal Herbage: Astrological Insights: Cannabis Universe: Volume 2

<u>Planetary Pot: Aligning with Astrological Herbs: Cannabis Universes: Volume 2</u>

Doctor Who Meets the Replicators and SG-1: The Ultimate Battle for Survival

Nightmare Mansion: Curse of the Blood Moon

<u>The Celestial Stoner: A Guide to the Zodiac</u>

Cosmic Pleasures: Sex Toy Astrology for Every Sign

Hydrocephalus Astrology: Navigating the Stars and Healing Waters

Lapis and the Mischievous Chocolate Bar

Celestial Positions: Sexual Astrology for Every Sign

Apophis's Shadow Work Journal: : A Journey of Self-Discovery and Healing

Kinky Cosmos: Sexual Kink Astrology for Every Sign

Digital Cosmos: The Astrological Digimon Compendium

Stellar Seeds: The Cosmic Guide to Growing with Astrology

Apophis's Daily Gratitude Journal

Cat Astrology: Feline Mysteries of the Cosmos

The Cosmic Kama Sutra: An Astrological Guide to Sexual Positions

Unleash Your Potential: A Guided Journal Powered by AI Insights

Whispers of the Enchanted Grove

Cosmic Pleasures: An Astrological Guide to Sexual Kinks

369, 12 Manifestation Journal

Whisper of the nocturne journal(blank journal for writing or drawing)

The Boogey Book

Locked In Reflection: A Chastity Journey Through Locktober

Generating Wealth Quickly:

How to Generate $100,000 in 24 Hours

Star Magic: Harness the Power of the Universe

The Flatulence Chronicles: A Fart Journal for Self-Discovery

The Doctor and The Death Moth

Seize the Day: A Personal Seizure Tracking Journal

The Ultimate Boogeyman Safari: A Journey into the Boogie World and Beyond

Whispers of Samhain: 1,000 Spells of Love, Luck, and Lunar Magic: Samhain Spell Book

Apophis's guides:

Witch's Spellbook Crafting Guide for Halloween

<u>Frost & Flame: The Enchanted Yule Grimoire of 1000 Winter Spells</u>

<u>The Ultimate Boogey Goo Guide & Spooky Activities for Halloween Fun</u>

Harmony of the Scales: A Libra's Spellcraft for Balance and Beauty

The Enchanted Advent: 36 Days of Christmas Wonders

Nightmare Mansion: The Labyrinth of Screams

Harvest of Enchantment: 1,000 Spells of Gratitude, Love, and Fortune for Thanksgiving

The Boogey Chronicles: A Journal of Nightly Encounters and Shadowy Secrets

The 12 Days of Financial Freedom: A Step-by-Step Christmas Countdown to Transform Your Finances

Sigil of the Eternal Spiral Blank Journal

A Christmas Feast: Timeless Recipes for Every Meal

Holiday Stress-Free Solutions: A Survival Guide to Thriving During the Festive Season

Yu-Gi-Oh! Holiday Gifting Mastery: The Ultimate Guide for Fans and Newcomers Alike

Holiday Harmony: A Hydrocephalus Survival Guide for the Festive Season

Celestial Craft: The Witch's Almanac for 2025 – A Cosmic Guide to Manifestations, Moons, and Mystical Events

Doctor Who: The Toymaker's Winter Wonderland

Tulsa King Unveiled: A Thrilling Guide to Stallone's Mafia Masterpiece

Pendulum Craft: A Complete Guide to Crafting and Using Personalized Divination Tools

Nightmare Mansion: Santa's Eternal Eve

Starlight Noel: A Cosmic Journey through Christmas Mysteries

The Dark Architect: Unlocking the Blueprint of Existence

Surviving the Embrace: The Ultimate Guide to Encounters with The Hugging Molly

The Enchanted Codex: Secrets of the Craft for Witches, Wiccans, and Pagans

Harvest of Gratitude: A Complete Thanksgiving Guide

Yuletide Essentials: A Complete Guide to an Authentic and Magical Christmas

Celestial Smokes: A Cosmic Guide to Cigars and Astrology

Living in Balance: A Comprehensive Survival Guide to Thriving with Diabetes Insipidus

Cosmic Symbiosis: The Venom Zodiac Chronicles

The Cursed Paw of Ambition

Cosmic Symbiosis: The Astrological Venom Journal

Celestial Wonders Unfold: A Stargazer's Guide to the Cosmos (2024-2029)

The Ultimate Black Friday Prepper's Guide: Mastering Shopping Strategies and Savings

Cosmic Sales: The Astrological Guide to Black Friday Shopping
Legends of the Corn Mother and Other Harvest Myths
Whispers of the Harvest: The Corn Mother's Journal
The Evergreen Spellbook
The Doctor Meets the Boogeyman
The White Witch of Rose Hall's SpellBook
The Gingerbread Golem's Shadow: A Study in Sweet Darkness
The Gingerbread Golem Codex: An Academic Exploration of Sweet Myths
The Gingerbread Golem Grimoire: Sweet Magicks and Spells for the Festive Witch
The Curse of the Gingerbread Golem
10-minute Christmas Crafts for kids
<u>Christmas Crisis Solutions: The Ultimate Last-Minute Survival Guide</u>
Gingerbread Golem Recipes: Holiday Treats with a Magical Twist
The Infinite Key: Unlocking Mystical Secrets of the Ages
Enchanted Yule: A Wiccan and Pagan Guide to a Magical and Memorable Season
Dinosaurs of Power: Unlocking Ancient Magick
Astro-Dinos: The Cosmic Guide to Prehistoric Wisdom
Gallifrey's Yule Logs: A Festive Doctor Who Cookbook
The Dino Grimoire: Secrets of Prehistoric Magick
The Gift They Never Knew They Needed
The Gingerbread Golem's Culinary Alchemy: Enchanting Recipes for a Sweetly Dark Feast
A Time Lord Christmas: Holiday Adventures with the Doctor
Krampusproofing Your Home: Defensive Strategies for Yule
Silent Frights: A Collection of Christmas Creepypastas to Chill Your Bones

Santa Raptor's Jolly Carnage: A Dino-Claus Christmas Tale
Prehistoric Palettes: A Dino Wicca Coloring Journey

If you want solar for your home go here: https://www.harborso-lar.live/apophisenterprises/

Get Some Tarot cards: https://www.makeplayingcards.com/sell/apophis-occult-shop

<u>**Get some shirts: https://www.bonfire.com/store/apophis-shirt-emporium/**</u>

Instagrams:
@apophis_enterprises,
@apophisbookemporium,
@apophisscardshop
Twitter: @apophisenterpr1
 Tiktok:@apophisenterprise
Youtube: @sg1fan23477, @FiresideRetreatKingdom
Hive: @sg1fan23477
CheeLee: @SG1fan23477

Podcast: Apophis Chat Zone: https://open.spotify.com/show/5zXbrCLEV2xzCp8ybrfHsk?si=fb4d4fdbdce44dec

Newsletter: https://apophiss-newsletter-27c897.beehiiv.com/

If you want to support me or see posts of other projects that I have come over to: **<u>buymeacoffee.com/mpetchinskg</u>**

I post there daily several times a day

Get your Dinowicca or Christmas themed digital products, especially Santa Raptor songs and other musics. Here: **https://sg1fan23477.gumroad.com**

Apophis Yuletide Digital has not only digital Christmas items, but it will have all things with Dinowicca as well as other Digital products.